Here is a candid, touchingly honest book on marriage as it is really lived. Poetic in form, these informal, unaffected "conversations with Christ" reflect the realities of Christian marriage in the day-to-day experiences of a husband and wife. Every Christian couple will be able to identify with the joys and sorrows, the major and minor incidents, the trials and tribulations of Joseph and Lois Bird.

The poems are divided into three sections—married love, children, and community. In the first, the authors reflect on the intimate relationship between husband and wife and consider with openness and sensitivity such topics as love-making, fatigue, and pregnancy. In the second section, devoted to life with their children, the daily vignettes range from the moving treatment of a daughter's surgery to a delightful reminiscence of a gift from a six-year-old. The final section, on the family's role in the community, is concerned with questions of world importance such as hunger and poverty as well as practical considerations on pornography and a hard-to-get-along-with neighbor.

Written with beauty and tenderness, Love Is All gives vivid witness to marriage as it is lived—with its ever-present problems, joys, and sorrows, and challenges.

LOVE IS ALL

Esther & Vic —
   In gratitude for
making it all possible —

         Patty & Stan

LOVE IS ALL

Conversations
of a husband & wife with God

Joseph & Lois Bird

IMAGE BOOKS
A Division of Doubleday & Company, Inc.
Garden City, New York
1973

Image Books edition 1973
by special arrangement with Doubleday & Company, Inc.
Image Books edition published February, 1973

These are for You, Jesus.
Thanks for being here
and listening,
always.

The two of us,

One

What a wild,
    crazy,
        wonderful
            life You've given us.
You've given us a dream
        . . . and a promise,
                a dream of beauty
                        and a promise of its fulfillment.

A wild,
    crazy,
        wonderful
            life.

You described the life You were calling us to.
        You said it was very good.
And it is,
        but that doesn't say enough.
And when we joined our hands, hearts, and bodies
        we had no way of knowing
                how good this life was to be.
We couldn't anticipate
        the wonderful world You were giving us.
We're dreamers.
        We freely admit it.
But what's wrong in dreaming?
Can there be anything more fun,

anything which gives more richness to our
                                          existence,
     than a dream?

We talk of our marriage
     and they call us unrealistic.
All right. We're unrealistic.
     But we don't want what they call reality.
We like the unreality
     of phosphorescent beaches,
          picnics for two,
               shared nights of rain,
                    and the touch of skin
                         warmed by an open hearth.
All of our life together has been part of the same
     unrealistic,
          crazy,
               wonderful dream.
During those first years

     we feared waking up.
What would happen to our dream world
     when we collided with the realities
          of sickness,
          conflicts,
          unpaid bills,
          pressures of housework,
          pressures of a job,
          demands of children,

                                   and all the rest?

Now we know.
And what a wonderful surprise!
We still have the dream,
     and it is now so much more vivid;
          it's become our own private reality.

It seems all so simple, Lord

and it is simple.
The answers to loving are never really hard to find;
        it's the loving itself which is often difficult.
When we tell them,
        they accuse us of oversimplifying.
But doesn't love have a kind of simplicity to it?
Why do they make it so complicated?
        And why do they call the dream unrealistic?
Is it because You are unreal
                in their lives?
The entire dream hinges on You.
Without You, there can be none.
You *are* the dream,
        and when You gave us Yourself,
                You gave us a wonderful dream,
                        one that's an idle fantasy, they say.

Lord, what are they talking about?
If love is unrealistic,
        nothing makes sense.

Without love, this world is insane,
        a biting,
                clawing,
                        screaming world of madmen.

Without You,
        this world is a cruel,
                meaningless, joke.

Without love,
        only the most courageous,
                or the most foolish,
                        would prefer life
                                over death.

We've seen the world they describe,

the realistic world,
the world without dreams,
                  without love.

And yes, it's real.
            Very real.
It's all the reality of hell,
            the reality of the death of everything.
Lord, it's like having your guts torn out
            and feeling your very soul shrivel
                              and decay.

We know that kind of reality;
            we've lived in that hell.
You know the times,
            don't You?
You've seen us slam the door on loving
            and turn our backs on the dream,
                              and on You.
And You've watched us go through the self-imposed
                                             torture
      of not loving
            or being loved.
                  And hell is the only word for it.

But that dream and that promise
            are the only reality we want.
They are the only reality of meaning
                              and joy
                              and sanity.

We know this.
We know we have to cling to it.
Lord, You've given it to us
            Don't let us lose it.
And we know we can't hide it away
            and selfishly try to keep it to ourselves.

13

We have to try to share our dream
        even when they call us unrealistic.
If we don't,
        we may lose it.
And somehow, dear Lord, we feel sure
        if we stay with You,
                the three of us can bring it to those
                        who have lost it.

Hang on, Lord.
We need You.
        Without You, we fall into that realistic world
                                they describe;
                                and we die;

we lose the dream,
and we perish.

Stay with us
        and help us stay with You, Lord.
That other world is all around us.
It seeps into our pores
        and eats away at us like a cancer.
Sometimes we forget
        how easy it is to lose the dream
                and how dead we are without it.

Help us to remember.
Lord, help us to keep the reality of You.
And help us not merely to say,
        "To hell with that other 'reality,'"
                but to see it as the hell it is.

You've given us a wild,
        crazy,
                wonderful
                        life—

14

a dream—
and a promise.
Please, dear Lord,
please help us to
keep it.

Two

We talk a lot about communicating,
but what do we mean by it?
Last night we threw away an hour or two
talking but not reaching,
producing sounds of irrelevance.
We phrased and re-phrased,
explained and clarified,
and said nothing.

We talked
but we didn't touch.

We tried to tie our feelings together with words.
They didn't work.
Or we didn't listen.
An hour or two we threw away
in a loneliness of syllables.

Why, Jesus, is it so difficult
to know each other through words?
Day after day we can be free;
We can know each other, unhampered,
and meet across a verbal bridge.
Then it collapses,
and language becomes a tangle.
But why do I ask?
Fear and self-interest.

Always, fear and self-interest
break down what we call communication.
We're so afraid to expose ourselves,
to strip our emotions naked,
to show what we are, what we feel,
to expose the fears, the doubts,
to reveal the anxieties and petty jealousies,
to give to another the picture of ourselves
which might bring shame
or a javelin of accusation.

What foolish fears, Lord.
What groundless anxieties!
We no longer need fear.
We no longer have reason to doubt one another.
Can it be that never can two trust fully
or love totally?

And the self-seeking.
The efforts to "prove points"
and win arguments,
to convince
but not to give.
This, far more than fear, erodes understanding,
doesn't it?
It eats away the roots of "knowing."

Dear Jesus, the temptations are so present:
The demand to be understood,
to be accepted.
The refusal to understand
or accept.

You've given us the gift of language, Lord.
Help us learn to communicate
It seems so very close to loving.

Three

Each day, Lord, we offer You
    our works,
        our sufferings,
            and our joys.
But today was pure joy!

We called a babysitter,
    and took the day off.
        Just the two of us.
It was a day we've repeated many times.
First, the drive into the city:
    sitting close,
    touching,
    watching people,
        and cars,
            and signs,
    talking of everything
        —and nothing,
    sharing thoughts
        —and cigarettes.

And then the city:
    our city,
        in the way we've come to know it best:
        walking, hand in hand,
        shopping the store windows,
        smiling at strangers,

browsing book shops,
strolling art galleries,
discovering that restaurant
that's "just right,"
and that flower cart with fresh violets,
two bunches: one for her coat,
one to carry
and laugh with.

It was our kind of day,
a day of romance,
laughter,
and wonderful foolishness.

A day of pure joy!
Dear Lord, may we offer You this day?
It's been a lot of fun!

Four

Scrubbing a floor
and making love on fresh cool sheets.
That's it, isn't it, Jesus?
They're both parts of a greater whole!
I learned that truth today,
not for the first time,
but again in a way that made it the first time.

I cleaned our house,
waxed our floors,
sorted,
straightened,
polished,
scoured.
And it was fun!
A love-making fun!

Lord, how could I view cleaning an oven as just
                                                            a chore?
How could I see scrubbing a floor apart from him?
Was I trying to divide love into separate pieces?
It can't be done.
And now I know.
Cleaning his house is also making love.

It also is part of the sacrament we share
and live.

Today, I didn't give my husband a waxed floor
or a cleaned window.
I gave him myself.

Five

What would I be without her?
What would I accomplish
or contribute?
Would I have courage?
Would I find strength?
Would I hold convictions?
Would I be anything
without her?

Could I be complete without her?
Could I find peace?
Or purpose?
Would the air I breathe,
the particle of space I fill,
the force that is my life,
the death that terminates it,
have meaning
without her?

Dear Jesus, You were a stranger,
a myth,
a fiction in pastels on a holy card.
Could I have ever met You
without her?
Would I have found manhood
or known womanhood
without her?

Those feelings that raise doubts,
those facets and dimensions of the total *me*,
would they have remained hidden and undeveloped
without her?

Could I have learned to love
or learned to accept love?
Would I have liked myself
or given to another?
Would I have found beauty
or discovered mystery?

Nurturing the seedling into a tree,
she brought the gifts of sun and rain
with her womanhood
and her love.

She is my wife,
the air I breathe,
the blood that flows in my veins.
Whoever I may be,
whatever I may become,
if there is goodness and joy and life,
it is hers.

Dearest Lord, You gave her to me.
And she introduced me to You.

Six

She was tired tonight,
     very tired.
It was in her eyes
     and in her walk.
Her footsteps
     . . . like the steps of pregnancy
     . . . the heaviness,
          the slowness.
But it isn't a child she carries;
     it's fatigue.
Tonight, its weight pulled against her back and calves
                    like the fullness of her womb at term,
     shifting her weight to her heels.

She was tired
     . . . and I wanted her.
I wanted to be near her,
     to talk with her,
     to watch her respond,
     coming alive,
     fresh,
     erasing the ache, the strain that tightened her
          face and pulled at her arms and shoulders.
I wanted her to turn off what she felt,
     and accept what I felt.
She came to me then,
     her eyes and voice

an apology: "I'm very tired."
Was it then?
Was it in my answer?
    The choice:
        not to love?
I put my arms around her,
    kissed her,
    encouraged her to go to bed,
        to rest,
        to sleep.
I said the words, and I kissed her,
    but what was in my voice?
Did I want the words to have meaning?
Didn't I hope she'd hear the disappointment,
    the plea to be loved?
Wasn't I saying, "Ignore your needs;

                        meet mine!"

I followed her to our bed,
    not at once,
    but too soon.
She wasn't asleep
    . . . but didn't I know she would be awake
    . . . waiting?
    Wasn't I hoping I'd been successful,
    that she'd know of my needs,
    my desires,
    my demands?
                Of course!

And I knew she'd lie beside me,
    head raised,
    leaning on her elbows, talking,
    brushing my hair with her finger tips,
    coming alive,
    using love as her weapon to fight fatigue.
                I knew!

Now, she sleeps. Her breathing: deep, and so very
                                                    slow.
She hasn't moved,
        not even to kick back blankets from her feet
            (she always says they need to "breathe")
But I can't sleep; I'm not even drowsy.
I'm disgusted
        with myself,
        with my selfishness,
        with my demands.
Lord, You know me. You know the depths of my
                                                    selfishness.
You see me, smug within my egocentric shell.
You love me.
        But tonight, I can't love myself.
She sleeps so soundly; and I miss her.
We're apart now,
separated by sleep.

She needs this rest,
        this sleep.
Love her, dear Lord,
        in the way I should have loved her.
She was tired tonight,
        so very tired,

                                and I wanted her.

Seven

Climbing out of bed each morning is simply awful.
  Throwing back the blankets,
  pulling my feet over the edge,
  lifting my shoulders,
  rubbing the scales of sleep from my face,
      seems such a severe penance, Jesus.
  Gravity plays tricks;
      the bed holds me
          and I sink deeper into the mattress.

"Good morning, my darling."
"Good morning, dear."

You've given us another day, Lord,
  but right now I can't appreciate it,
                not enough.

The sun is shattering, screaming
  through our bedroom window.
  I close my eyes,
      but no use.
  A sun, bright red,
      remains behind my eyelids.
But it's a beautiful day,
  a day with promise,
      and expectations.
Too bright, perhaps,

but it has laughter,
even though greeting it, I have little.

The hills, and our lone olive tree
are alive.
And we're alive.
Thank you, Lord.
We're alive, and awake
—almost,
partially.
They're all waiting for us—
the hills,
the olive tree,
our children.
Your world has been waiting while we slept.
And, Jesus, I like Your world.

But throwing back these blankets is awful.
I know I have to.
That world is out there,
and I have obligations.
But getting up,
that means something else.
It means telephones,
and diapers,
and leaving for the office,
and people,
and activities, and forces, and pressures,
and all sorts of things which keep us apart.

And so I delay;
I procrastinate;
we both do;
and I pull the blankets close.
We hold each other
and try to shut out thoughts of time.

But, dammit, it still passes,
    and it's getting late.
We're going to have to hurry;
    breakfast will be rushed.
Yet knowing that, we still hold each other;
    still shut out the world
        . . . for just a little longer.

Lord, please,
    give us just a few more minutes,
                just a few.

Eight

Today I looked at brown grass,
watched a gray squirrel,
tall trees,
a bouncing rabbit,
the flame of a match.

Today I saw a field,
a reservoir,
blue,
a hill
of rocks,
slates and browns,
an ancient bush,
robins and dusty clouds.
And today,
I saw my husband's face.

Today I listened.
I heard the counterpoint of dawn,
babies calling me,
children
dressing in noise and movement,
coffee perking,
strong men and trash barrels,
the sounds of doors,
eggs boiling,
the rain of acorns.

Today I listened.
And today,
I heard my husband's voice.

Today I smelled toothpaste,
a wet diaper,
fresh yellow mums,
a child's vomit,
damp newsprint,
seat covers,
turned earth,
coffee steam,
and the ocean.
And today,
I smelled the fragance of my husband's skin.

Today I felt the warmth of sun,
wine grapes,
sheer stockings,
a child's hair,
thick blankets,
sand,
and caressing breezes.
And today,
I felt my husband's skin.

Today I tasted fresh crab,
old smoke,
the tears of a child,
fresh bay leaves,
salt on an egg,
bitter tea,
and cold wine.
And today,
I tasted my husband's lips.

Today I looked

and listened;
I smelled
and tasted.
I came alive.

Today,
I lived.
And for today, I thank You.

Nine

Lord, something happened.
I don't know what.
But something happened,
      and we're apart.
Was it a word,
      a gesture,
            something unspoken?
Was it anything so small?
Could it have been anything of so little importance?
Could anything have been that important?

Here we are:
      Saying,
      and doing,
      polite things,
      meaningless things,
      things which only make us more aware
                        of our separateness.

My God, what happened?
One minute the world seemed good.
      There was joy
      and love
            and we were close.
And then it was as if a light went out.
Was it me?
      Did I stop loving?

33

I don't want to accept the blame.
      Maybe that's why I don't see it.
But was it me?
      Did I pull away?
      Am I the guilty one?
Or is it important
      to know who failed?
What difference does it really make?
Right now, I only know we're apart.
      And Lord, it's awful.

We go about the things
      that must be done,
      all the necessary
      routine things,
            activities of unimportance.

We pass each other;
      we smile;
      we speak.
          But we're strangers.

There's a deep gulf between us,
      and a terrifying distance.
We both know it's there.
      We may deny it,
          but we know.

Lord, these feelings are ugly.
I feel lost.
And empty.
And dead.
      And I don't know how
          to find the way back.

Or maybe I do know.
Perhaps I'm afraid.

Perhaps it's that first painful step
                that frightens me.

But why?
What am I afraid of, Lord?
      Of being hurt?
      Of feeling rejected,
             unloved?

Am I fearful that this separateness
      exists only within me;
          am I afraid to find
             that it's a lack inside?
Or is it a fear of admitting failure?
Is that what keeps me silent?

Lord, it aches.
It hurts like hell.
It *is* hell
   —of course it is.
You are love;
I know You are,
      and if hell is separation from You,
         then this feeling,
         this agony of emptiness,
            must be hell.

Lord, I feel cut off
      from all love.
And I'm lost.
Lord, do You hear me?
I'm lost,
      and it's all so dark
         and cold.

Jesus, she must be hurting too.
                Isn't she?

She must want to reach out,
    to touch,
    to love,
    to be loved,
        as much as I.

But there's such a chasm between us,
    a pit, vast and deep,
    of darkness
        and fear.

Lord, help us.
    Please help us.
Give us Your hands.
Draw us close.
    Bring us together again.
Dear Jesus, listen to me.
    Please.
    I'm begging You.
Look at me, Lord.
    Can't You see how it hurts?
I'm crying inside
    and I'm dead.
We're so far apart,
    so very, very far.
        And it hurts like hell.

Ten

I had work to do,
deadlines to meet,
numerous tasks and obligations
that had been waiting.
But they're still waiting.
Tonight, I turned my back on them.
Tonight we made love.

And there have been other times,
times when there were chores ignored,
times we've sat together
holding hands,
drinking coffee,
talking of odds and ends
and wonderful things of little import
and much love.

Times we've watched our work grow in neglect
and tower as an avalanche
while we shared a sunset.
Without regret, we've lost awareness of time
while we've lost ourselves in dreams.

Once, Lord, I may have seen it differently,
perhaps, as irresponsible.
One time, annoyance might have followed
                        (at myself, always).

I might have cursed my weakness
and lamented my laziness.
But not now.

I've learned, Jesus.
Now I can see it as loving.
Now I can recognize that nothing can be more
                                        responsible,
or more important,
or more authentically You.

Why is it, dear Lord, that we can be intelligent,
                                        yet stupid,
perceptive, yet blind?
How do our values fall in irrational orders?
How could I ever have placed activities of things,
unnecessary and unimportant things,
above an offered moment of loving,
an opportunity to share?

Through You,
and with her,
the vision has expanded.
Now, so much more, I can see; I can judge
                                        importance.
Now I can weigh the moment.
Tonight I turned my back on the work, the deadlines,
and I chose to love and be loved.
And I was right.

Eleven

Dear Lord, today is our wedding anniversary.
It's a day filled with gratitude.
One of Your days.
> We offer it to You.
> > And thank You for it.
It's a day of memories
> skipping through and over years,
> > appearing,
> > > vanishing,
> > > > and reappearing.
You've given us those years;
> we've given each other those memories.

They've been very good years, Lord,
> full, exciting years.
But more important,
> they've been years of growth.

How much has happened,
> how much our life has changed,
> > and how much we have changed
> > > during these years.
There are those who say adults can't change.
> But we have changed.
Our values,
> our views of marriage,
> > our love,

our feelings for things, and happenings,
have all changed
and grown.

Back then, we didn't know,
we couldn't know,
the plans You had for us.
And we didn't know
the growth that would come from loving
and becoming one.
We were so afraid.
But what did we have to fear?
Responsibilities?
Sacrifices?
The loss of our separate identities?
How foolish we were.
How much we lacked faith.
Could we really ever have been that afraid?

I look at our wedding photographs
and I try to re-create that day.
But I can't.
Could we have been that couple?
That bride and groom,
they're so young.
But it isn't their youth.
I feel I don't know them.
They're not us;
not now.
Everything's changed.

It's funny, Jesus.
You gave us the answers,
right from the beginning.
But we didn't listen very carefully.
We squandered time
and energy.

We stumbled around,
        stepped on each other,
                and listened to silly advice:
                        "Develop mutual interests."
                        "Find a hobby you can share."
                        "Learn to communicate."
                        "Seek outside activities."
                                All the bits and pieces
                                        of very silly advice.

The growth came from You.
        It was You all along.
We heard it was to be a great mystery.
        It is.
                And with each year the mystery deepens.
It's You.
You've been the catalyst.
Why do we keep trying to take apart the mystery?
The mystery is love,
        and we can't analyze it
                because it's You.
We can try to know You;
        we can strive to listen,
                attempt to understand what You're asking.
But we can't analyze You.
        And it was You all along.

Those wedding photographs.
How You must have smiled at that boy and girl,
                                even laughed.
And how often You must have laughed
        during these years.
                We've even been able,
                        some of the time,
                                to laugh at ourselves
                                        and our childish fears
                                        and follies.

Each anniversary, dear Lord,
    is a day of nostalgia,
        a day sprinkled with memories,
            a day with special closeness,
                a day of hope.

Thank You, Jesus,
    for these days.
However many more years,
    or days,
        or hours
            You give us,
                each will be a very bright,
                    lovingly wrapped,
                        anniversary gift.

Twelve

I take so many things for granted,
    and forget to say, "Thank you."
I touch again and again the familiar memories,
    like fingers over a smooth-worn rosary,
        taking pleasure,
            but offering little in gratitude.

This bed, for example.
    The memory of a furniture store
        on an afternoon before our wedding.
    The confusion of those days,
        the tension,
        the pressures,
        those last-minute preparations.
    How little I knew her then.
    How superficial my love was.
She wanted a firm mattress;
    I didn't.
    I knew I could sleep only on a soft one.
And so
    we compromised,
    or rather, I gave in.
    And yes, it was a "giving in."
        I hadn't yet learned:
            "giving in" isn't giving.
It's funny.
    I don't think the bed is any less firm today;
                     perhaps it is.

Now, it seems it always would have been my
choice.

You gave a special benediction to this bed.
Our marriage was consummated
on it.
Our children were conceived in love
on this bed.
(Not all of them perhaps;
there were vacations,
weekends in the city,
afternoons on a beach,
evenings by a fireplace.)
We've cried, both of us,
on this bed.
And we've laughed.
We've been unloving,
and we've hurt each other.
But we've also loved.
Most of all,
we've loved.
And we've felt You very close to us
as we've held each other
and joined our bodies
on this bed.

I've been cold, chilled by fear,
watching her in pain
on this bed,
cursing in frustration,
praying in desperation,
feeling helpless.
And I've reached out to her,
pleading to be held and comforted,
becoming a child again in sickness
on this bed.

This bed has been an altar;
    these sheets,
        our altar cloths.
It's been a sanctuary
    where we have renewed our commitment.
We've found truth
    and beauty.
We've prayed
    and embraced in sleep
        on this bed.
It's been a retreat,
    a private chapel,
        and a mirror
            for Your love.

Thirteen

Why can't violets bloom all year?
You've arranged everything so well.
For all seasons, You've planned surprises.
Wildflowers in Spring,
snowfalls of yellows and blues;
full harvests of color in Summer,
pouring over spillways of gardens and forests;
Fall's crimsons and umbers,
feathering yellowed lawns.
And even the Winter days:
Firs and Spruces, blue-green
(with whip-cream topping).
A wonderful plan.
But why can't violets bloom year-round?

She carried violets on our wedding day.
Only violets, a single bunch.
No trailing white ribbons
or lily-of-the-valley garnishes
to add—what?

A hand of violets
clutched against a white-bound book.

They were the beginning.
Now, dried and pressed,
a purple fragrance encased in love

and locked away in nostalgia.
They were the first.

How many violet bouquets?
The birth of a child.
A dinner date.
An afternoon stroll in the city
(with a fresh wet scent from a flower cart).
And all those special occasions
which became "special" because there was no
occasion,
only violets
and her eyes alive.

But violets have such a short season.
Can it be only a few days?
There have been other flowers for her.
Mums, a single rose, carnations in red and white,
when violets weren't in bloom.
Yet they're not violets,
and violets are her.
Why can't they bloom all year?

Fourteen

I feel trapped by the boundaries of my skin,
    the limits of my senses,
        trapped and locked in
            by the separateness of my world.

I want to love him completely;
    I want to share his skin,
        feel with his senses,
            lose my identity in his.
But there is always a distance, Lord,
    sometimes of my making.
I can draw away,
    and I do,
        in selfishness
            or fear.
I can deny him my presence
    and my love.
But I haven't,
    not this time.
We're close, and we love,

    yet there's still a distance.
We live in unique worlds,
    worlds which are apart,
        worlds which are closed off and closed in
            by our skin.

We communicate;
    we hear each other;
        we understand.
Words cross the space between our worlds;
    they enter, and find acceptance.
Yet it isn't enough, Lord.
    The distance is still too great.

The joy and the pain are one, Lord;
    the joy of loving,
        and the pain of separateness.
I want to know that pain in his arm
    as he knows it.
I want to feel the raindrops
    that strike his forehead
        as he feels them.
I want his desires,
    his hungers,
        his satisfactions,
            and his frustrations
            to be mine.
But I know, dear Lord.
    It can never be complete.
My love must always be imperfect.
Our worlds can touch,
    but never merge.
That total oneness will come only after death
                             in You.

But help me, Jesus.
There are ways to love him
    I'm not seeing.
There are opportunities
    I'm avoiding.
Show me, Lord, how to cut down the distance.
    Show me the steps to take

to make our worlds less separate,
　　　less egocentric.
Show us the world
　　we can share in You.
Dear Lord, I want to be him;
　　I want him to be me;
　　　I hate these boundaries of skin.

Fifteen

I can't help it, Lord.
I need him so.
I reach out,
    call him back from wherever he is,
    call him to fill my world,
        a world empty without him.

Dear Lord, his world is filled.
    So many people,
        lovely people,
        hurting people,
            things,
            demands,
            commitments
                stuffed and crammed into minutes,
                        rupturing time.

And so few moments for us,
    so few fragments of time
        in which to share our dream.

Does he miss me, Lord?
Does his world fade gray
    and chill with winds of vacancy
        when I'm not there?
Does he feel the longing,

the pull that wrenches deep inside
        with fingers of fear
                and pain?

I can't believe he does.
He makes the choices of involvement,
        and extends the limits of his world.
He adds pieces to his existence
        while I watch him go away.
But my world is him;
        I have no other
                and I crave none.
So I can't believe he misses me
        in the way I long for him.

Is it that I am a woman
        and his world is the world of a man?
I wouldn't trade it, dear Lord.
        I've no envy of his world.
My world is free
        in a way his world is not.
In my womanhood, You've given me a freedom to love
                                that he cannot know,

        and a security in love
                which comes through him.

Would I want him changed?
No, not when I'm truthful,
        not when I look at him,
                not when I admit my needs
                        and the security I find in what he is.
Would I want him less involved,
                less concerned,
                less responsible?
Of course not!
He is a man.
        Would I wish him less?

I could build a separate world, Lord.
　　I could fill it with commitments
　　　　　　　　and involvements.
I could shape my world
　　in the image of a man's.
Then I might not miss him,
　　but I would miss the gift of love.
There is a pain in our loving
　　that deepens and enriches the joy of our loving.
Our oneness increases the pain of each moment apart
　　and magnifies the joy of each moment together.
I want no other life.
But sometimes I can't help it, Lord.
I need him so.
I reach out to clutch a star
　　and cry in pain when its heat burns my fingers.

Sixteen

All day I've thought of her,
thought of her in paths that wander,
pause in reverie,
and wander on and back.

All day she's appeared
and reappeared,
sprinkling memories.

The touch of woman flesh.
Sounds of breathing.
Her breast cradled in my hand
in the night,
her nipple, a fledgling,
snug in the nest of my fingers.

All day.
The rain smell of her hair.
Little girl sounds of love.

All day
we've been apart;
all day we've been together.
All day,
she's been here
        with me.

Her eyes,
wide in the pains of labor,
closed in the infancy of sleep.
Eyes that burst sunrise
and crash ocean waves
        of anticipation.
Eyes that retreat and wash gray
                        in anger.

Her eyes.
Eyes that look out on her world.
Eyes with the goodness of laughing children
and the wickedness of dancing daydreams.
Her eyes.

All day I've thought of her.
The soft taste, sweet,
of her mouth,
the taste of fresh cream
cooled by well water.

Her mouth, a pink softness.
So much
her mouth.

All day.
Her thighs,
the feather touch of her thighs.
Her feet touching mine;
        love, in syllables of one.
Her laughter.
Her cries.
Her arms
        lifting our baby.
Her hands
        caressing my body.

55

Fragments of years,
stored in a treasury of love.
Mementos of morning songs,
                    evening sighs.
Souvenirs of flowers;
        memories of midnights.

All day I've thought of her.
Her face: a pirouette:
                a girl,
                a woman,
                child,
                lover.
And she is mine,
a part of me.
My body is hers,
my life, her life.

All day.
That voice, her voice:
in words of love,
whispers of silence,
murmurs of joy.
A poetry of truth.

All day, I've heard her voice.
I've listened to it echo the sounds of promise,
gifts of grace
and prayers of love.

All day, dear Jesus, I've been aware of You.
You brought her to me.
You stood to hear our pledge of love.
She placed her life in mine;
        we joined our lives to Yours.

All day my thoughts have been of her.
And being of her,
        they've been of You.

Seventeen

It won't be long until he's home.
A little while, and then we'll be together.
It's been a sweet, long day, a day of waiting.
Soon, Jesus, I will hear the sound of his car,
his key in the lock,
and the waiting will be over.

I'll know when I see him
which thoughts to share
and which to cherish quietly alone.
It's always hard to remember,
when he's seemed so close all day,
that my experiences have not been his
and his have not been mine.
So much, it seems, that everything is shared.
Our life is so much *one*, that I forget.

Dear Lord, I have to look to him.
Today he may have had one of those days
when the words "I want you" could only add to his
tiredness.
Soon, I'll know.
I'll know if I can share with him the feelings in
my body,
the fantasies of longing for him.
I'll know which parts of my day to give him:
the odor of freshly ironed clothes,

the fun of handling his things,
the new cupboard arrangement,
the pictures and sounds of my life joined to his.

I used to feel awkward when I wanted him,
embarrassed, perhaps,
and unsure of his reaction.
But no longer, Jesus.
I've learned of loving
and the freedom of love.
Through You, and him, I've found the beauty and
                                              virtue in our sexuality.
Now I thrill in thoughts of our love,
in images of his body
and its maleness.
Now I can accept and enjoy the desires I feel for
                                              him now
and take pleasure in the fulfillment of yesterday's
                                              desires.
I can be warmed by pictures of his face above mine,
silhouetted black by the sun,
memories of an undiscovered beach,
our bodies touching all over,
in the nudity and sanctity of love.

No hesitation or awkwardness now separates us.
I know his body as I know my own,
and as he knows mine.
Through loving, I can now accept the luxury of my
                                              womanliness
and the excitement of his maleness.
I can accept being loved
as well as loving
and the fun of loving.
The freedom.
The oneness.

The feeling of being whole.
Dear Lord, it's good!
Loving him, and wanting him, is so very good.
And in a little while, the long day of waiting will end.

Eighteen

We made love last night
    and today is new,
        brand new
        and alive.
The air vibrates,
    fresh with the odor of first rain.
The world this morning is all color,
    rainbows of people,
    sounds,
        and surprising, wonderful things.

We made love
    and everything was re-created.
Our marriage began again;
    it was a wedding night,
        a radiant white wedding night.
Again, last night,
    with our bodies we said "I do,"
        "I take you as my husband."
        "I take you as my wife."
It was all repeated
    last night.
And it was all new
    last night.
As if for the first time,
    we consummated our marriage,
    conceived our children,
    committed our lives.

Again, we held each other,
    joined our bodies,
        and entered an always-new world
        in which man and woman become one.

With this wondrous gift You've given us,
    we closed the doors and windows
        on the world of everyday.
For a while, everything stopped—
    people,
    telephones,
    chores,
    demands,
    worries,
        all ceased.
For a time, the dead skin of our days,
    the calluses of trivia that dull our senses,
        peeled and sloughed off.
We were born again
    to each other.

We breathed deeply,
    filled our lungs with the fragrances of love,
    listened to the music of its sounds,
    its crescendos, its shifting tempos.
And we touched.
With our hands, we spoke to each other of love,
    communicating with the sensations
        offered and received.
With our lips, we formed the words of love;
    and tasted the richness of each other,
        savoring the flavors of love.
All that we are, and all we hope to become,
    as a man,
    as a woman,
    we gave to each other
        as our very essences flowed and blended.

61

Every act of love
    became that single act of love.
Every day, every year of our marriage,
    every joy, every sorrow,
        all that has been our life in love,
                we relived last night.
We talked,
we laughed,
    and we prayed together
        with our bodies.
And You were so very present.

It's then that You always are,
        especially then.
Our closeness to each other
    increases and makes more alive
        our closeness to You.
You're there.
    It's Your love—
    It's You—
        blending, merging, fusing us
        into the beauty of unity
            with You.
And You were there as we fell asleep,
    our bodies entwined,
    the warmth of our love
    curling in and about,
        forming in a prayer
            of thanksgiving and hope.

And this morning?
    This morning is sunrise,
    and growing things,
        and feelings of anticipation.

Today is new,
    brand new

and alive,
and the spiral of our love-making goes on,
    drawing us together
               upward,
        toward You.

. . . our children,

Nineteen

I can't think about children, Lord.
I can think only of a child.
Each child.
Our child.

There's Paul.
We've known him longest.
Our first-born.
Paul, with the gentle hands,
the pouting lip,
the swimmer's legs.
Paul, with eyes for distant birds
and ears that hear Your voice.
Paul, with the messy room
and the loving soul.

And Ann.
Our golden one.
So tiny still,
and yet big in kindness.
Ann, who reaches out
and clasps the world in her small arms.
Ann, so unable to grasp the hurting
and being hurt,
so eager to become a woman,
so much a woman now.

Susan:
So quick to giggle
and to storm.
Sunbeams and clouds
in brown eyes.
Susan, with the art of feeling
and the feeling for art.
Susan, with her daddy's eyes,
with music,
guinea pigs,
and giggles.
Susan, who shrugs at life
and laughs.

Then Kathy.
You know her.
She loves You so very much.
And she knows You.
She shares You with us
in her teasing
and her tears.
Kathy, a child of joy.
Kathy, who says "God loves me,"
and says it with a certainty.
Kathy, of long legs, blue eyes,
and love.

Or Joan.
So quick to coax
or cuddle,
offering an eight-year-old heart.
Joan, accepting her role of in-between,
tolerating those older,
indulging those younger.
Moving in and out of so many worlds.
Joan,
beguiling,

67

manipulating,
annoying.
Joan, a leprechaun and a princess,
an in-between age eight.

Each child, dear Lord, a different gift.
Unique, and each a part of You.
Not children, plural,
but each child.

Stephen, the oldest of the little ones,
so self-assured,
looking like his father.
My Stephen who liked to rock.

Or Mike, flexing a four-year-old's muscles,
fearless and funful,
creating a circus of confusion.
Mike, who has taught me much.

Mary, the wind-up toy
with a round tummy
and a big voice
and hair that never stays combed
and feet that seldom stop moving.
Mary: seldom silent, never sad,
an antidote for boredom.

Diane:
Our youngest,
running on uncertain legs,
treasured by brothers and sisters,
imitating,
demanding,
currying attention with shyness and smiles.
Diane, our baby.
Different and delightful.

So much herself.

Nine children.
A family.
But I can't think of children, Lord.
I can think only of a child.

I can think only of Paul.
I can think only of Ann
                or Mike
            or little Diane.
Each child.
Our child.

Twenty

I'm not pregnant now, Jesus.
And the fullness seems far away
  in time,
    though it isn't really so long ago.
Now, I'm a little more restless,
  a little less patient,
    and yes, not even quite as contented.
There's a lush fullness that comes with pregnancy.
  And a sureness,
    a valley of security
      that comes with being full
        of his love.
It brings a period of waiting,
  of quietude,
    of time without importance.

We went to church this morning, Lord.
And I watched pregnant women
  and heard the cries of a new born.
And, dear God, I ached.
I envied them, Lord.
  Their swollen awkwardness,
  The inconvenient sleeping bundles
    in their arms.
I envied them.
  And I prayed for them.
I prayed that they might know
  the joy I've known,

70

that they might feel that closeness,
    a closeness that comes with pregnancy,
        a feeling of oneness with You,
            with my husband,
                with the earth and all growing things.

I prayed that they would cherish their time of waiting,
    that they would find new goodness
        in themselves,
        in You,
        and in their husbands,
    that they would be given courage and faith
        to live each day during that time of waiting,
        and to live it fully,
            without waste.

I wasted so much, Lord.
    You know just how much.
So many times, so very many,
    I pretended not to see You.
So many times
    I screamed at You.
In frustration,
    I denied my belief in You.
And it was only slowly,
    after so long a time,
        so many lost opportunities,
            that I came to know.
And even then, it was in bits and pieces,
    small insights into myself,
        my marriage,
            and my womanhood.
Gradually, the pieces formed in a mosaic
    of self-knowledge.
This was one of Your gifts.
    Have I ever said, "Thank You," Lord?

Then, but not before, was I able to recognize this
                                        need,
        this desire I feel
                deep within me,
                        as a woman,
                                to be impregnated by my husband.
Only then, could I see clearly my need
        to carry him in my body,
                not only his child, but him,
        to see him
                and You
                        in the faces circling our dinner table,
        and to find in this living love within my body
                a living expression
                        of the trinity in my vocation.
It's like making love,
        isn't it, Lord?
Pregnancy is very much like making love.
Only in carrying him and his love within me,
        the union of our sexual love lasts longer.
It's as if the heights of our love-making
        continue on in richness
                and fulfillment
                        for a full nine months.
And that's why the ache comes,
        isn't it, Lord?
That's why the feeling of emptiness
        after I deliver a child.
        The child is in my arms
                but I feel vaguely restless
                        and lonesome
                and there's a greater need
                        to touch and be touched,
                                to make love to my husband.
During those months of waiting,
        those days of growth,

I live with the lush fullness
          of his love,
                    and Yours,
                              inside me.
For every minute
          of every day
                    until our child is delivered.
And then,
          afterwards,
                    for a little while,
                              I'm lonesome.
Are these strange thoughts, Lord?
          Perhaps neurotic?
Are they loving needs,
          or needs to love?
I feel the emptiness, Lord.
          And a conflict.
                    It's a conflict I've known before
                              and, dear Lord, it can grow
                                        and become terrible.
One day,
          one minute,
                    the desire for that union without time
                              is intense,
                                        compelling.
The next minute
          reason,
                    physical comfort,
                              and yes, even selfishness
                                        drive my feelings and thoughts
                                        far back.
I try to avoid my feelings,
          try to run from them.
                    But I can't run fast enough.
I know the way out, Lord.
This morning, when I prayed for those women,
          I was praying for myself.

All along, I've known the way out of the conflict:
 I have to seek him
      and You.
           I have to seek love.

Twenty-One

A gift from a six-year-old
doesn't come with a price tag.
And that's one of the things which makes it
                                    wonderful:
It's priceless.

A scrap of paper
scribbled with crayon,
the bloom of a weed,
a building block castle:
     "Shut your eyes, Mommie and Daddy;
      I have a suprise for you."
And there it is:
His heart—
wrapped in a smile.
No bartering.
No strings.
No reservations.

There's nothing impersonal
in a six-year-old's gift.
All that he has,
he gives.
That, and all that he is.
That drawing taped on the kitchen door

is his gift of You,
and his offering of him.

I can learn a lot, dear Lord,
from a six-year-old.
His gifts have no price tag.

Twenty-Two

I know what I'm supposed to be.
I know my responsibilities, Lord,
and I welcome them.
There are times, however,
when I become discouraged.
Times like this.
The obligations of fatherhood all seem so much
                                    —too much.

I look at my children
with wonder
and gratitude.
Then I look again,
and I see myself.
I have doubts, many doubts,
and fears.
How do they see their father?
Do they see a man?
Do they find convictions?
Strength?
Courage?
Or only weakness?

They're growing.
They're forming values and interests,
developing habits,
shaping pictures of the world.

They have a picture of me, Lord.
Each different.
But I haven't seen those pictures,
and probably never will.
Would I wish to?
Would I like those pictures?
Could I take any pride in the fatherhood they see?
Would I find that they have known You
                              through their father?

I don't like facing these questions, Jesus.
And at times like this, I don't like the answers I give.
More often, I don't ask.
I just avoid.
I shut my eyes,
keep busy,
distracted,
comfortable.

But then these moments come.
Times when all else stands still
and I'm left with only You,
You, and my fears,
You, and my naked self.
Times that come at night
and push back sleep.
Times driving alone in a car,
or kneeling in church.
Those times.
Then it's always the same.
I want to go to them,
tell them I'm sorry,
tell them of my failures,
give them my promise
       to be the father they deserve.
Sometimes I do,
       but too seldom.

Sometimes I ask their forgiveness
            but never enough.

I scold too much,
demand too much,
shout,
berate,
and ignore
        too much.

Dearest Jesus, You've given me a responsibility.
It's awesome.
Frightening.
And I don't do very well at it,
        not very well at all.
I needn't wonder how they see me.
I know how I see myself.
And there are times,
times like this,
when I don't like what I see.

Twenty-Three

I'm not sure what I'm feeling right now.
    Anger, perhaps,
    or resentment,
    or frustration.
I know I'm afraid,
    tied up inside
        like shoe-lace knots.
    My jaws ache
        from clenching.
Lord, I don't like these feelings,
    but I can't seem to work my way through them.

I took our baby to the hospital today,
    carried her into that cold pastel maze
        of hurrying people in cardboard white,
            people who don't know her,
            people who can never know her
                            as we do,
            people who smile
                and say polite, expected things,
            people who refer to her by her last
                                name
                or by a diagnosis and a room
                                number.
But I'm wrong to feel resentment.
There's a kindness at that hospital
    and Your love among the staff.

It's just that she's our baby,
 and so little,
   and they can't know her as we do.
Tomorrow, she'll have surgery.
 Not serious, the doctors say,
 and we have confidence in them.
 But still, it *is* surgery.
And I have these feelings;
 I want to slam my fist into the wall.
Is it You?
Am I angry with You?
I think so.
I can't make sense of all this.
 Why must it be our baby?
  Why not me?
  I can endure pain.
   Not well, perhaps,
    but at least I can understand why
        I hurt,
    and I can fight, and complain, and
        swear,
   and I can even,
    should I choose,
     turn my suffering to virtue.
 But our baby can't,
  and that's why I'm angry.
And I can't explain the hurt to her.
I can't tell her why we must leave her
 in a strange room,
  to sleep in an unfamiliar crib,
   beside other babies who hurt.
I can't tell her there's some meaning in it
  because I haven't found any meaning—
   not in the suffering of an infant.

I want to understand.
I tell myself You love us,

You love her.
I want to believe some meaning,
  some purpose,
  can be found in her suffering.
But I can't.
  Or I won't.
  Or I haven't tried hard enough,
          or prayed long enough.

Are You talking to me?
Is there some meaning here You're trying to show me,
          something I'm shutting my eyes to?

Lord, where are You?
I can't see You
  or hear You.

I need You.
She needs You.
I must believe in Your love for her;
          I have to.

Lord, don't go away.
  Please don't go away.
I know I lack faith.
I doubt.
I demand reasons.
  And I become angry with You
          and with myself.
But that's me
  and my impatience
  and lack of faith
      and trust.
Pay no attention to my weaknesses.
          Not now.

Just care for her.
Please, Jesus.
  Please.

I'm helpless to do anything.
I can't hear You,
      but I have to believe
          You can hear me.
Lord, I can't make sense of it.
I'm angry,
      and I keep asking "Why?"
                     "Why?"
But that's unimportant.
Lord, listen to me!
Please, Jesus,
      please hold her.
Don't let her hurt.
She's so very little.

Twenty-Four

The children are returning to school,
   another vacation so soon ended,
         and Lord, I'm going to miss them,
            especially this time.
It isn't always this way;
   my feelings aren't always this good,
         this loving.
Knowing me, You know that,
   don't You, Lord?
Sometimes I'm quietly relieved
   to see them go.
Sometimes I welcome the peace
   and order of an unfilled house,
         the quietness of babies napping,
            the freedom of space unoccupied.
But this time it was different.
This time I tried,
   really tried, Lord.
This time I prepared for the vacation
   and made ready for my family.
I prepared our house,
   anticipated our shopping,
         even planned our meals
            in readiness for a vacation of joy.
But most of all, Lord,
   I prepared myself.

It was my windows that needed cleaning,
 the windows of my soul
  that needed the dust washed off
   to let in their sunshine.
My rooms were in need of their fresh air,
 the clean breeze of their laughter,
  and, yes, even their quarrels.
And it was my housecleaning,
 the preparation of me,
  that made it so different.
They know You, Lord,
 and they love You.
  Even when they joke about You,
   they know
    and love You.
But then, You know that too.
For a brief time, dear Lord,
 with no homework,
  no hurrying,
   and no outside "musts,"
    they were able to share You with me.
How alive and real You then became.

Something wonderful happens at these times.
It's as if You walk in the door
 and all the lights go on.
Faces shine laughter
 and words become raindrops of sunshine.
And dear Lord, the world of a home turns to fun,
 a jumping-up-and-down,
  hugging-one-another
   world of fun.
We're a family!
And, dear Jesus, there's nothing can touch us
 when we're a family.
It's everything of joy,
 everything of love,

and, so much, everything of You.
The wonderful happened.
We were closed in,
        bound together,
                but not by an exclusiveness,
                        by love,
                                and a time without pressures.

Our love grew,
        love for You
                and for one another.
And with it,
        our family grew
                and expanded into the world.
How can I say "thank you"
        for such a vacation?

Now it's over
        and I have to watch them return to school,
                watch the pressures again build,
                        watch,
                                always,
                                        the hands of a clock.
The clocks are here again, Lord.
        And I'm going to be forced to watch them.
There's a danger in it.
        I've seen it before.
        I've fallen into the trap before.
                Too often, I've watched a clock
                        and missed seeing You
                                or them.

But today, Lord,
        after a vacation of fun
                and a family of love,
                        I know it doesn't have to return
                                to a world of clocks.

86

It can be vacation joy
        next week,
                and next month,
                        and this morning.
And a clock can be a "thank you"
        for one more minute
                of opportunity,
                        one more moment of love.

Twenty-Five

Lord, it's easy to be close to You on Christmas Eve,
                                        very easy.

To know You're here
        with us,
        sharing our fun.
To feel You
        surrounding us,
        encircling us,
        warming us,
        drawing us closer to each other
                                and to You.

We don't open our gifts Christmas Eve.
        That's for morning,
                along with Nativity Mass,
                        singing emotions,
                                and Your birthday cake, Jesus.

Christmas Eve is wrapping time.
        It's children sleeping,
                almost,
                hopefully.
        It's gifts out of hiding
                (each year more a challenge),
                plastic, battery-operated toys
                        (mentally marked: *expendable*),
                new clothes,

and always, one to-be-assembled item
(Crosspiece G passes through A and is
secured by wingnut H to side B.
Patience, Lord, please!)

The base of the tree becomes hills and valleys,
a jumbled landscape
of colored paper.
Always so much,
so many presents.
Lord, I forget;
You've been so generous.
The final wrappings,
more hurried,
less aesthetic,
more functional.
But children like unwrapping presents,
so every gift must be wrapped.
"Have you seen the tape?"
"I think it's underneath that red paper."
"Will you hold this ribbon while I tie?"
"How does one wrap anything shaped like this?"
"There, that's the last of them."
"You know, I think this is our prettiest tree ever."
"I know, but we say that each year."

It's late now,
well past midnight.
A long, fun, look before flicking off the tree lights.
A long look
and just one glass of wine.

To bed, morning will come early.
But not to sleep,
not right away.
It's been a wonderful evening,

an evening full of wonder
and love.
And we're tired,
but we don't want it to end,
not just yet.
We hold the moment,
lie here in the darkness,
clinging to the feeling of bright bubbles,
warm,
laughing bubbles.

Our bodies touch,
but never enough.
Never.
"Merry Christmas, darling."
"Merry Christmas to you, my dearest."
And a Happy Birthday, Jesus.
Thanks for joining us tonight.

Twenty-Six

I had a headache this morning. I woke up with it.
It wasn't the blinding or splitting kind
    . . . nothing so dramatic
    . . . just the squinting-at-the-light-and-gritting-
                      teeth variety.
Knowing myself, the headache should have put me
                      on guard.
    It should have warned me like a yellow caution
                     light.
                     But it didn't.

I screamed inside while I cupped water in my hands
    and dipped my face in it.
    With my palms, I tried to press the hurt
            from behind my eyes.
I should have seen what was coming
    and turned to You.
I should have asked Your help,
    should have thought of Your pain
    when they pressed thorns into Your head.
But I didn't.
No, instead I clung to my annoying little headache
            and wrapped myself in pity.

What a repertoire of excuses I have.
    One for every occasion,
        every challenge,
        every choice.

I need only reach into my mental file and pull
                                        one out.

Today, it was my headache.

When I went down to breakfast, it happened.
                    (I guess I knew it would.)
I greeted my family with my headache,
        welcomed the new day
            with impatient shouts.
I berated my daughter to tears,
        barked demands,
        and deserted my wife
            for a newspaper.

I knew Your voice was there.
        I didn't want to hear it.
And even if I had heard You,
        I probably would have whined my excuse:
        "Lord, You don't understand. My head hurts."

But that's one of the things that hurts even more.
I have no excuse,
        because You do understand.
            Your head once hurt.

Twenty-Seven

Soon, she will be eight years old.
    And eight is a wonderful age.
        School still has a newness,
        there's a universe for exploring,
        and doors of words open on other people
                        age eight.

Clothes are fun at age eight,
    little girl clothes,
        every bit the clothes of a young lady,
            proper and starched on Sunday,
                with white gloves,
                a hat that never stays on,
                and a purse
                    that treasures
                        a broken pencil,
                        a plastic toy,
                        a piece of ribbon,
                        a handkerchief,
                        and a penny.

Eight is an age of awareness,
    an age of tiny wildflowers
        and giant climbing trees.
It's an age of knowing You
    without fears
        or complications,

an age when tears explode without
warning
storm for a moment,
then wash into laughter.

Being a father has special rewards
when your daughter is eight years old.
You're still on a pedestal,
a king and a god,
uneasy, perhaps,
and unworthy,
but still it feels kind of good.

Her eyes see the perfect father,
the ideal lover,
the healer of all hurts,
and the absolute authority
on everything.
It's a good age for a father,
a very good age.

The eight-year-old birthday always brings an expected
gift,
a planned for,
dreamed for,
eight-years-of-waiting-for gift.
At age eight,
a bicycle,
a brand new,
all your very own,
full-sized bicycle.
And that, too, is a special reward
for the father of an eight-year-old.
Five times I've shopped for a bicycle,
compared construction,
questioned durability,

and made a choice on sentiment
and color.
Black and white for Paul.
Blue was Joan's color.

But this year there will be no bicycle.
And this year there'll be no eight-year-old birthday
cake
to be decorated by Daddy's sugary art.
My eight-year-old daughter won't be here
to ride the new bicycle.
There will be no birthday party,
no pink and white wrapped gifts,
no boys and girls circling eight candles.
This year,
as last,
and the years before,
she will spend her birthday with You,
Jesus.
I've spent no birthdays with her, Lord.

Her daddy has never decorated a cake for her,
or watched her run,
or held her on his lap,
or kissed her hurts away.
I've had no chance to warm her bottle
or change her diaper
or tease her to laughter.
Eight years she's lived with You.

Eight years we've been apart,
and yet we know each other.
She is my daughter,
a part of me,
and I am her father.

I know her through her mother
    and in her brothers and sisters.
And they know her,
    not as a space of lawn
        marked by chiseled marble,
            but as their sister.

She prays with us,
    rejoices with us,
        and sorrows with us.

She lives with You, dear Lord,
but in the way that only a father can know his
                                    daughter,
                I know her.

I don't know
    or really care
        what theologians or philosophers say it's
                                    like there
                                    with You.

I see my daughter,
    my eight-year-old with the frilly dress
        and the little white gloves.
You've been her father
    for eight years,
        and You know her too,
            know her and love her
                as a father loves his very feminine
                    eight-year-old daughter.
And You know about eight-year-old birthdays,
    and brand new bicycles,
        and cakes decorated by Daddy.
So You see, Jesus,
    while I miss her,
        and the eight-year-old birthday party,
            and shopping for a brand new bike,
                and decorating a cake,

I know she'll have a happy
                birthday,
a very extra special
eight-year-old
happy birthday.

Twenty-Eight

It was a heavy, warm day,
    wet
    and hot, really hot,
    with cross children.

I moved, crawling, dragging myself, through time,
    doing many things,
    chores and necessities,
        not very well,
           dodging,
               . . . avoiding involvement.

I made it. I remained detached
    from their sweating,
    sometimes sticky,
    clutching fingers.
    They reached out,
        but I wasn't there.

Oh, I met their demands all right . . . (Didn't I?)
    I heard their voices,
    listened to their complaints,
    mediated their squabbles,
    dried their tears,
        but all through a thick fog
                of petulance.

I didn't choose *to be*,
    didn't want *to be*
      . . . for anyone.
And so I made the choice.
I moved through time
        alone
            . . . untouched.

I filled my day to overflowing
    with things:
        uninteresting things,
        unavoidable things,
        chores, obligations, requests
        met grudgingly in justice,
            but not in love.

I smothered in a sandpile
        of things
    . . . petty, dull trivia.
The obscenity of still another day passed,
           merely passed,
        discarded like ugly waste;
        and another day before me,
          and then another.
Lord, what has all this to do with loving?
    Nothing.
    You knew;
        and so did I.
    I rejected Your gift of this day,
    walked away from Your challenge,
    refused Your cross,
    and shaped my own
        out of self-pity.

There must be another way, Lord.
Why don't You challenge me,
    really challenge me?

Why don't You test me with real fire?
Then at least I could say,
     "It was too big,
     or too hard,
     or too painful."
Why won't You make my cross grand enough
          that I can take consolation
          when I fall.
Lord, I'd like, just once,
     to believe I failed
               heroically.

Why must I always fail in pettiness,
in laziness,
and in all the small, momentary,
     lost opportunities
               to love.

Why must I fail
     in responding
     to a child's voice
     or in sweeping a floor
          for the umpteenth time,
     or in resentment
          when he retreats to his newspaper?
Why can't I choose a different way
               in which to love You?
Perhaps,
then,
I could love You more.

Let me try something else, Lord,
     at least for a time.
I'd like a vacation,
     a vacation
     from being
     me.

I'm far too lazy,
　　　too stubborn,
　　　　　too petty,
　　　　　　　too selfish
　　　　　　　　　to love You
　　　　　　　　　　as I am.
Just for a little while,
　　　a day or two,
　　　I want *to be*

　　　　　　　　. . . someone else.

Twenty-Nine

Dear Lord, I need Your help
                    now.
I need it very much.
It may seem trivial;
        and in a way it is.
It's no major crisis,
        no serious problem.
I'm just tired.
        Dead tired.

It's the sort of exhaustion that builds up,
        gains in heaviness
                and slowness.
The energy of breathing
        becomes a conscious force,
        rationed in sighs
                and collapsing yawns.
It flows like a sap
        into my arms and legs,
                coagulating in my joints.

This is more than the end of a day.
This is a fatigue of several days and nights,
        days of too much work,
                nights of too little rest.
And now I'm paying the price:
        I'm so very, very tired.

I don't think I can go on another hour.
Late afternoon,
    and I'm only half alive.
Lord, I'm beat,
    and I'm going to need Your help.

I've tried all my usual tricks to come awake:
    splashing cold water in my face,
    gulping fresh air,
    moving around,
    biting my lip,
    drinking coffee,
        but nothing helps.
            I'm worn out,
                and unless You help,
                    I don't think I can make it
                              through.

This evening is important, Lord.
Our daughters are in a school program,
    one of the twice-a-year performances for parents
        with music by the elementary orchestra,
        poetry recitations,
        and selections by the school choir.
        A very important evening.
Three of our daughters are in that program
    and they expect me there;
        they expect both of us.
And we both want to be there,
    sitting side-by-side,
        holding hands,
            picking our children out from among
                      the others
                (always the best looking),
                    feeling very much married,
                        very much their parents.

Lord, I don't want them to look over that audience,
        find me,
            and see only tiredness.
I don't want them to see a lifeless face,
        perhaps to see it as boredom
            and conclude that only an obligation holds
                                me there.
Because it isn't merely obligation,
        not even the obligation of love.
I want to be there.
I'm proud of our children,
        and proud that it's important to them
            that I be there.

So tonight, Lord, I'm going to need Your help.
If You prop me up
        and bring me awake,
            I can give my family this evening;
                I can give them myself.

I don't want to be merely conscious;
        I want to be alive.
        I want to love them.
        I want to be present,
            fully present,
                for them.

Hold onto my hand, Lord.
        Hold on tight.
I need to be turned on tonight.
        But I'm so tired,
            so very tired.
You're the only one who can throw the switch.
        Please don't let me down.

Thirty

Marty, a little boy,
    with a face of sun
        and eyes that search to tease,
           sat on our kitchen floor.
He laughed,
    he chattered,
        played with our children,
           and brought them a wonderful gift
                    from You.
When You made Marty,
    You gave him no arms,
        and a leg deformed.
Yet we saw no cripple in Marty.
We saw no lack, dear Lord.
His smile is grace;
    his laugh, a prayer,
        and Marty is whole, in You.

He sat in their midst,
    playing their games,
        holding their eyes with the dexterity in his
                    toes,
        catching their envy and awe.
He sat, wrapped in love,
    wealthy in it,
        free with it,
           scattering it like handfuls of jewels.

How can I describe what he gave?
Can one describe a flower?
Or the sky?
Can Your love be put in words?
When You made Marty,
You gave him no arms,
but You gave him much more,
and You made him whole.
And Marty, with his face of sun,
sat on our kitchen floor,
sharing that gift with us.

Thirty-One

Being a father, dear Lord, means taking risks
    and then living with the pains of doubt.
It means pondering,
    weighing,
    making decisions
        and then facing the fears.
Watching them falter on a new bike,
    thoughts of speeding cars
        and broken limbs.
I give a Christmas gift,
    an archery set,
        but all my words of caution,
            all my admonitions,
                can't erase my fears.
He wanted a rifle,
    not a real one that fires bullets,
        but one that uses compressed air
        and shoots pellets.
It was the only thing he asked for.
    "It could be for my birthday and Christmas
                      both," he said.
    And, Lord, I know what he was feeling.
        I can remember
            that special gift,
            the waited-for,
            deep-down longed-for
                special gift.

So I bought the rifle,
    placed it in his hands,
        and showed him how to fire it.
But, dear Lord, I had to wrestle with myself on this
                                  one.

More than the bicycle,
    or the archery set,
        it has me scared.
I don't like guns,
    but it isn't that.
It's just the danger,
        and the responsibility I've placed in his
                        hands.

Am I afraid of trusting him, Lord?
        Is that it?
    Do I want to keep him a child?
    It is easier,
        so much easier,
            to say, "Wait until you're older,"
            and, to myself, "Wait until your father
                  has no fears."

I can't do that though, Jesus.
I have to let him grow.
I can't hang on to him
    and escape my fears
        by denying him responsibility.
I've seen too many
    smothered by protective walls.
He doesn't have to prove anything to me,
        only to himself.
And I can't lock him in childhood.
But I'm still scared, dear Lord.
I can't see that rifle without thoughts,
        terrible thoughts,
            touching off the fear again.

Then the doubts return,
    all the memories of poor decisions,
        the follies and mistakes of a father.
If only there were fewer,
    perhaps the fear would lessen,
        but I'm so very often unwise.
I made the decision, Lord;
    I took the risk,
        and the responsibility rests on me.
But I need Your help.
I placed a rifle in his hands.
        And now I place him in Yours.

Thirty-Two

I'm running away, Lord,
        hiding myself
                here in the bathroom.
But it's not really running away.
It's just that at times,
        not often,
                I want to be alone,
                        away from the endless questions
                        and demands
                                and needs
                                        of my family.
So it isn't running away,
        merely retreating,
                and only for a few minutes.
I need this time alone.
        Don't I?
Shouldn't there be some free moments,
        some time each day
                when there are no voices
                        and no demands,
                moments during which to meditate,
                        to play with thoughts,
                                or just simply to relax?
Certainly, I should be entitled to this much.
        Shouldn't I?
I mean, is it asking too much
        to have these few minutes?

A few minutes alone
        and I can summon energy,
            gather my thoughts,
                and turn them back to them
                    —and to You.
I really feel it's wise
        to take this time.
It's for them too.
I can be kinder,
        more attentive,
            and in every way more loving
                with these few minutes alone.
Why, then, do I feel guilty?
I shouldn't.
And why do I invent reasons
        to excuse myself
            and retreat from my family?
I shouldn't need to.
And most of all, Lord, why do I argue this with
                                    You?
        Somehow, I feel I'm trying to convince You.
            But why?
Is it because I have doubts?
I must have;
        I always lose these arguments with You.
I can lock out everyone,
        the whole world,
            even my family.
                But not You.
                    That's why my arguments fail.
I didn't come in here to think
                or meditate
                or even refresh myself.
I came in here to escape,
        to run away from the challenges.
How long doesn't matter.
        I'm ducking out on my responsibilities.

That's all there is to it.
And I've been lying to myself
    and to You.
I'll unlock the door now.
But keep kicking me, Lord.
    I do a lot of running away.

Thirty-Three

I saw our baby today.
I looked at her,
    at *her*,
        and I saw not just a baby,
            not just one of our children;
                I saw *her*.

For an instant,
    I saw her—
        whole,
        complete,
        wrapped in all that is human,
        formed in light,
        turned in Your image.

For that suspended moment
    I saw her,
        glimpsed her mystery,
            and I understood.

Only You, Lord, know the secrets:
    Who is she?
    What is she to become?
    What plan have You for her,
        this child we call Your sister,
                     our daughter?

You alone, dear Jesus, know,
    and yet in my arrogance
        I forget.

I intrude,
　　poking with fingers of selfishness,
　　　　and try again to mold her
　　　　　　more in my image
　　　　　　　　than Yours.
What pride consumes me?
What vanity permits me to see her as a possession,
　　and ignore her as the gift of a whole person?
What evil in me views her as a responsibility
　　yet blinds me to her as a privilege?
What assumptiousness grips me
　　when I fumble to shape and manipulate her
　　　　as if Your gift is raw clay
　　　　　　placed in my clumsy hands?
Mold her in Christian living?
My God, what appalling arrogance!
Do I have so little faith in You?
You have created her in Your image, dear Lord.
Help me to see *her*
　　in the completeness of Your creation.
Help me to create an atmosphere of love,
　　an environment of You,
　　　　one in which she can grow in the beauty
　　　　　　　　　　　　of You.
Lord, deliver me from the temptation
　　to mold her,
　　　　to form her in my misshapen image.
Lord, I cannot shape Your image; I can only distort it.

Today, I saw our baby.
I saw *her*,
　　whole,
　　reflecting of You.
Tomorrow, I may again be blind.
　　　　Help me, Jesus,
　　　　　　help me.

. . . and the world.

Thirty-Four

Lord, tonight we had plans.
We wanted it to be one of "our evenings,"
and we planned it:
    an early shower together,
    wine,
    Christmas tree lights,
        and closeness.
But everything fell apart.
The doorbell rang.

The whole evening,
    everything we planned,
        was lost.
            The doorbell sounded
                and company arrived
                    unexpected
                        and, to be truthful,
                            unwelcomed.

We lost the evening we planned
    but now we can't even regret it,
    at least not entirely.
Someone needed us
    and it was good to be able to be here
    and to offer them whatever we have to offer.
I'm sure You had something to do with this evening,
                                Lord.

You gave us an opportunity to give ourselves.
And if we had closed that door,
we would have closed it on You.

Lord, we've learned that offering a cup of water
        to one who thirsts
                can be a gift to You.

But how much more
        when we give something of what we are,
        when we reach out,
        offer our help
                or guidance
                        or, perhaps, only our sympathy.
Then, the thirst which is quenched is ours,
        and the gift we receive
                overshadows our giving.

We may have lost the evening we planned
        but we found something,
                and for this
                        we thank You.
And we discovered something, Jesus:
        "Our evenings," when we are able to have them,
                become much more
                        because of these evenings
                                when the doorbell rings.

Thirty-Five

It's Advent,
    and through the long purple days of Advent,
        the days of anticipation,
        of penance,
        of preparation,
            we wait.

Waiting can be a unique kind of misery.
What anguish they must have felt during those long
                            dark years
after the fall,
    years spent watching for the star,
    years during which their hopes faltered,
    and their faith barely flickered
            in the darkness.
Longing so for the coming of the Light,
    what pain that waiting must have been.

How much of my life is spent in the frustration of
                            waiting.

    Waiting and hoping,
    waiting and dreaming,
    waiting and praying:
        the slow months of pregnancy,
        the first word spoken by a child,
        his first step,
        the new furniture,

the oft-postponed vacation,
the hours we're apart.
And I'm impatient, Lord,
so very impatient.
I need to learn patience, Lord.
Or perhaps I have learned it;
I just don't practice it enough.
But more than that,
I need to learn how to wait;
I don't do it very well at all.

Too often, my periods of waiting
are used only for waiting,
nothing more.
They're times not of my movement,
only the movement of a clock.
Too often, they're times without meaning
or growth,
and, worst of all,
they're times without love.
I don't plan time,
or use it;
I sit, like a lump of clay,
and let it wash over me.
I complain of the ruts,
yet I keep digging them,
and I make my todays worthless,
my tomorrows endless.
I squander my days
as if assured of living forever.
Lord, You asked Your friends to wait one hour
with You.
Help me learn how to wait.
Help me turn my times of waiting
into times of Advent.
Help me learn to use time,
not merely fill it.

Help me to stop vegetating,
    and start growing.
Help me to *work* toward Your kingdom,
    not just *long* for it.

Help me to hold precious the time You've given me,
    to live as if this minute is my last,
    to see, and grasp, my opportunities.
Help me, in the purple of Advent, to discover Your
                        meaning
                          in waiting.

Thirty-Six

We think of the island, Jesus.
Our island.
We know every foot of it,
every grain of sand on its beaches,
every broad-leafed tree, every flower,
every wave that washes it.
We've walked its shores hand in hand.
We've bathed in its sunlight
and slept by its surf,
climbed its trees with our children,
listened to its night sounds.
It has been our island,
ours alone.
You know it, don't You, Jesus?
We've talked of it with You,
shared it with You.
A daydream?
Perhaps.
But not really.
Our island is real,
so very real.

Our island has no telephones,
no drop-in guests,
no neighbors with fences and trimmed lawns,
no social commitments.
There are no clocks,

121

no calendars,
no letters to be answered.
There are no faces of pain,
no voices calling.

That couple sitting across from us,
their marriage, broken bits and pieces of rubble
piled deep about their feet,
are asking for answers,
for help.
Perhaps they're listening;
perhaps not.
They've been hurt,
deeply,
and they want to run.
Are they, too, seeking an island?
They ask something of us.
What is it?
And do we have what they seek?

Our hands reach out;
we touch each other;
and we're together,
on our island.

A photograph of a child
in a magazine:
withered limbs that curve like a spider's,
the swollen belly of starvation,
and those eyes.
My God, those eyes:
vacant,
wide,
saying so much,
pleading for so little.
Can we fly away to our island?
Can we take him with us?

The dinner party:
Correct, well-lacquered people.
People who see us as strange.
Secure people.
Frightened people.
Insulated people.
Lonely people.
We open our mouth to speak,
but there are no words.
We try to listen,
but not enough.
"It's been a delightful evening.
Thanks so much for inviting us."
And we run to each other
—and our island.

Appointment books,
stuffed with notes and coded commitments,
names, dates, and times,
forming in the doors of a trap
and the walls of a cage.
Why, Jesus?
Why does it need be?
How does it happen?
Do we build the trap with our own hands?
Does everyone build a trap
in which they're caged,
clawing at the walls,
dreaming of their island?

Our island is each other, Jesus,
the two of us and our children,
forming a circle,
closing out the world.
Is it wrong?
Is it selfish?

123

How often we've talked, dear Jesus,
of running away to our island.
We have our island in each other,
but we've talked of another kind of island,
a place away from all voices, all faces of pain.

Is it wrong to want to leave a world
walled in by telephones and time,
to leave it
if only for a little while?

You went into the desert.
Remember?
Were You, too,
perhaps searching for an island?

Are we each, in our way,
struggling to be free?
Does every man, every woman,
long for an island?

We have our island now.
We find it at night
in each other's arms.
We walk its beaches
with our children.
Are we seeking too much?
Is it unjust,
unloving,
to want still more?

Show us, dear Lord,
the world You've given us.
Show us the place for our island,
the direction we must follow.
Tell us, once more,
what we owe to others.

Are we trying to run away from them?
From You?

If we are not to fly to another island,
help us keep the one we have,
the one we rediscover when our hands touch.
Show us how to save our island
when that sea of telephones
and clocks
rushes in.

Thirty-Seven

Today, Jesus, I've been bored.
I don't know why.
Some days take wings,
today moved as a turtle.
My work was dull,
and as the day crawled it worsened.
It became meaningless.
But why?
Today was no different from other days.
Activities were no more tedious,
no more demanding.
Yet today was boring and endless.
And I don't know why.

Were You ever bored in Your work?
When You were a carpenter at Nazareth,
did You ever feel You were sawing the same boards
and nailing the same planks
over and over?
Do most men, at times, suffer boredom?
I think so.
And somehow, I feel You must have.
Perhaps it's a part of being human.

But, Lord, there's something that bothers me in this.
I can't quite dig it out,
but it's there.

I think it may be a temptation that follows the
                                              boredom.
I withdraw.
I don't try as hard.
I don't give as much.
I'm not as present to those who need me.

Is it because I'm bored?
Or does the boredom follow only when I'm giving less?

Thirty-Eight

We talked to a group of teen-agers.
We talked to them of life and sex,
marriage and loving,
of being a man,
and being a woman.
We talked to them of becoming.
And, dear Lord, they're beautiful!

They're vital,
filled with wonder and questions,
brimming with conflicts and hope.
Searching for answers,
clawing down stockades erected of clichés
                    (mortared with bigotry).
And finding what?

They're beautiful, Jesus.
Nakedly honest.
Frightening in insight.
We look into their faces, and it becomes an
                    examination of conscience.

We have failed them.
We, their parents, their teachers,
have betrayed them.
We've talked an ideal which we haven't lived.
And they know.

They're trying to live an ideal; we've lived only words.
Words, platitudes, mores, and proprieties.
Words upon words upon words.
They stand before us,
holding a mirror.

We spoke with them
and they listened with skepticism
and doubt.
(Was there cynicism?)
They were guarded; we expected it.
Yet when they talked, they accused.
And we, the elder hypocrites, are guilty.
We beg their forgiveness,
and Yours.
We've mouthed virtue, and given them a world of vice.
We've sought pleasure, avoided pain, and ignored love.
What greater sin could we commit.

A wall separates us, Lord.
We're afraid of them.
Their eyes penetrate our façade
and we wince with shame,
then lash out to criticize their world.

Perhaps they're unsure of their goals.
(Have we defined our own?)
They may not have found the answers.
(Have we paused to ask the questions?)
But they seem to be seeking Your world,
and rejecting ours.
(Is it this which disturbs us?)

Jesus, we need them;
We need their questions
to become our questions.

We need their hope
to rekindle our own.
We need their concern
to dispel our apathy.

And they need us,
not as we are, but as we should be.
They need our support,
not our suppression.
They need our faith,
not our scoffing.
They need our experience,
not our censures.

Dear Jesus, we need each other.
We need a freedom and acceptance
to bridge the gap.
Only as one family, in You, can we find hope.
Help us, Oh Lord.
The distance seems so great,
our generations so far apart.
Help us, through Your love,
to close the gap.

Thirty-Nine

The phone rings or I receive a letter,
    another request for commitment
        and involvement,
            Christian involvement, they say,
                outside my home.

Each time, Lord, I must go through it all again,
    all the questions,
        all the answers,
            all the sorting of duties and desires,
                all the reasoning and rationalizing.

Each time,
    all again,
        every time I am told of Your need for me
            out there.
Where is my place, Lord?
    How am I to best serve You?
What am I to answer to these involvements,
    these organizations,
        these activities,
            outside?
Each time I am challenged,
    I face the same questions.
Is it loving
    or lack of loving?

Is it responsible
        or irresponsible?
Am I a good parent
        or an indifferent parent?
Is it my selfishness
        or my convictions
                which keep me in my home
                        or draw me outside?
Each time, the same questions.
        And each time, I must listen for Your answers.

Perhaps this time, Lord, the answers will be different.
Perhaps this time
        I am wiser
                or stronger
                        or the need greater
                                or my responsibilities less.
Perhaps this time
        I can justify
                (or rationalize)
                        this outside involvement.
Perhaps this time
        it isn't an escape
                and a shirking of responsibility.
Perhaps this time
        it's a Mothers' Club
                or a parish group
                        and I can feel that I'm a better parent,
                                and that my family will truly benefit
                                        by my involvement.
But it's not this time
        is it, Lord?
Not this time.

Dear Lord, why do you let me glimpse a family
        that expands and reaches out
                to include the whole world

132

when my world seems so small
and my part so minor?
There's so little that's grand
and important
in my life.
I won't receive any medals
or applause
for diapering a baby
or loving my husband.
But that isn't important to me
I enjoy my world.
I'm not seeking for anything else.
But perhaps that's part of the conflict.
Am I being honest?
My enjoyment, the joy I find in my home
and family,
makes me feel somehow slightly guilty
when I am told I should become
involved
outside.

Each time, Lord,
I have to find the answers
all over again.
Perhaps next time
the answers will be different.
But not now.
I know what You've given me, Lord,
and what You've asked of me.
I have but one vocation,
one life to which You've called me.
And I can bring the world to You
only with, and through, my husband.
Through our marriage,
our oneness,
we speak for You.

You've shown us the way.
You've let us see
    that a Christian world
        is given birth in a Christian home.
Help me to remember this, Lord,
    when that phone rings
        or that letter arrives.
Sometimes it's hard;
    and I forget.

Forty

I was in a hurry, Lord,
and he did look like a common tramp:
    unshaven,
    clothes old and stained,
    a face trampled by weariness
                  (and pain?).

He said he was hungry,
but he begged only the price of coffee.
And he looked at me.

But I was in a hurry, Lord.
I looked away.
I didn't want to see him;
          not then.
I wanted to shut him out
    as one turns from the sight of a dead animal
                      beside the road.

I couldn't run,
    but, Jesus, I wanted to.
I wanted to run from all the hungry men,
    all the begging children,
    all the pleading women
        suckling starving infants
            at barren breasts.
I wanted to run

back to my antiseptic world
    of scrubbed children,
    scented women,
    and well-pressed men,
        polite men who never beg—
            and never hunger.
But I couldn't.

We walked to a restaurant.
We ate together
and I listened to the pain in his voice.
In his eyes, I saw the crucifixion.
    I saw the lashes of injustice
    from the faces that turned away.
And I saw myself
    in shame.

Dear Jesus, how close I came
        to walking on.
Sure, I was in a hurry,
but how could I have failed
    to recognize Your face?

Forty-One

There was this meeting, Lord.
People, gathered together,
protesting injustice.
People concerned for the rights of other people
with pigmented skin
and other people who speak with accents
and labor in fields
and sleep in tar-paper boxes.

There were speakers, Jesus.
Men asked our help
and spoke Your name.
They asked us to right these wrongs.
But somehow, Lord, it didn't come off.
We should have left with a different feeling.
We should have walked out with a new resolve,
        a re-commitment to our brothers.

We should have gone forth, again into the world,
          singing,
            our arms about each other.
But we didn't.

Did You notice, Jesus?
On one side, a group of Negroes talked together.
In a corner, several nuns huddled in whispers.
Farm workers, dressed in dust and Spanish lyrics,
        gathered toward the back.

Everyone, so polite,
              so very polite.
Words and phrases,
Songs and prayers,
              of justice.
(Presuming, we even spoke of love!)
All very polite.
Words
              upon words
                      upon words.
The new unabridged proper Christian lexicon!
Mine eyes have seen the glory of the new vocabulary!

No offense intended.
No offense taken.
All very proper, considerate, polite.
All very ecumenical.
A priest.
A rabbi.
A minister.
A labor leader.
And a politician.
But it just didn't come off.

It's so very easy, Jesus,
to love people
     fifty,
        seventy-five,
            five hundred miles away.
Let them be out of sight,
let them be a photograph on a poster,
and I can bestow justice.
Let them have less,
        and I can love them.
Let them be hungrier than I
        and acceptance comes.

At a distance, they pose no threat.
At a distance, they can be my brother.

But walking across a room can seem impossible.
And loving a next-door neighbor can be hard.
Tonight, we took the easy way.

Forty-Two

I ate too much this evening,
    and I'm stuffed.
I feel almost bloated,
    disgustingly uncomfortable,
        a little drowsy,
            and somewhat ashamed of my gluttony.

I led my family in thanking You when we sat down
                                    to our table,
    but wasn't it, for me, merely a routine,
        a momentary delay
            in appeasement of my hunger?
                I'm afraid it was.

I didn't pause to think of Your last meal,
    of those around You on that Thursday evening,
    of the wonder and anxiety Your words must
                            have caused,
    of the pain and fear You must have felt
        when You told them what was to come.
Nor did I think of the gift You gave us at that meal.

And I didn't think of the others,
    Your brothers, and mine,
        who have no food,
        who have never felt filled,
            have never sat down to a table heaped with
                                    food,

have never tasted human kindness,
never broken bread in Your name.
I'm ashamed, Lord.
I didn't express any gratitude for Your bounty,
for the healthy children circling this table,
for the woman You've given me,
the woman who prepared this meal in love.
Bless us, Oh Lord . . .
and a belated thank you.

Forty-Three

He's an old priest—
and he's rigid.
They call him conservative,
some say reactionary.

I tried talking with him
of You
and people
and a changing world.
But our words kept stumbling over years,
and banging into semantic walls.

Today, he doesn't fit in.
His world is vanishing.
The church he has served is growing.
Ideas emerge, blowing winds which chill him.
And he's left alone,
standing in a crowded solitude.

He's an old-fashioned priest,
living in the memory of an old-fashioned world.
Reluctant,
suspicious, perhaps, of innovations,
dubious of a new vocabulary
and a new freedom.

Before, his life had security,
the comfort of days

repeated like a litany.
His vineyard had limits;
it had structure.
He cultivated
and tended
and worked toward the harvest.

About him, there were the good people,
people he knew
—not well,
but in the ease of roles
well learned.
A community circled by a rosary,
warmed by votive lights.
Infants were baptized;
old men were fortified for death.
He gave them peace;
they returned respect.
And, in a way, a love was built,
a love without pain,
a love without disturbing questions.

Now, dear Lord, he's uneasy.
Is it fear
or the pain of loss?

He's a good priest, Jesus,
and a very good man.
But he's being left behind.
They're not listening to his voice.
They're moving
    —perhaps without direction
    —perhaps toward truth.
    Only You can know.
    But they don't look back.
And he's being left behind.
In the well-worked rows of the vineyard,

he stands alone
  —and lonely.

Dear Jesus, help us find the way to love him.
Help him accept our love.
We need him.
We need his goodness.
He's served You well
and loved us well.
We need him at our table,
taking his place in our family.
We need him as a father,
as a teacher,
as a man with Your voice,
                Your hands.

Help us, Lord, to show him
what You have shown us.

And most of all, Jesus, help us see
what You have shown him.
He's an old man,
older than time,
rigid,
and lonely.
But You've taught him to love.
And he's a very good priest.

Forty-Four

We're in near darkness, Jesus.
Somewhere out there,
    the storm has blown down a power line.
And now,
    our neighborhood is in darkness.
No television,
    no electric clock,
        no refrigerator,
            no electric blanket.
                But worst of all, no light.
Now we have only the dim flicker of two candles.

Funny how much we rely on these things, Lord.
Funny how they make us feel secure,
    wrapped in the safeness of a home
        and a neighborhood of friends.
Somewhere a wire breaks,
    we're in darkness,
        and the long-forgotten fears of childhood
                                    return.
Quickly, stumbling, we light candles,
    but they give little light
        and their glow creates foreign shadows
            and unfamiliar shapes.
The candlelight returns only a portion of our lost
                                    security.
What a weak hold we have, dear Lord,
    on faith and courage.

Security in a copper wire!
Faith
    in an incandescent bulb!

We take You so for granted, Jesus.
We stay smug and secure in our neighborhood
    with electric lights
        and running water
            and tax-bought services.
And we cut ourselves off from You.
    So many times, we cut ourselves off from You,
        and we aren't even aware of the severance.
You,
    the only light we have,
        and yet we let a power failure frighten us!

There they are!
    The lights are on again,
        the lights, and the quiet hum of the
                  refrigerator.
The other houses on our block are warm again
    and electrically friendly,
        and all because a copper wire has been
                  mended.
Only a half hour of darkness,
    but the returning light turns everything to new.
                        Safe.
                        Secure.

What a fool I am, Lord.
I needed a power line failure
    to remind me of You.

Forty-Five

Only You, my God, know the time I have left.
Perhaps this breath is my last.
Maybe I've shared with her a final kiss.
For the last time, I may have spoken with my children.
Perhaps never again will I watch the sun turn red
                                    or feel the touch of love
                          or breathe the scent of evergreen.

Can I fear death, Lord?
Can I hold regrets?
Is there something more I can ask in life?
Everything,
no, more than everything
has been mine.
This woman,
these children who call me father,
those who have taught me,
those who have learned from me,
and, always and ever,
Your love.

If I knew I had only one more day,
what would I choose to do?
How would I fill that twenty-four hours?
Would I go to them
and tell them of my love?
Would I come to You to beg forgiveness?

Would I curse the moments lost
or protest the work undone?

Dear Lord, if I've lived, really lived,
the days You've given me,
they know of my love.
And if I've answered Your call,
Your forgiveness is always with me.
No moments will have been lost,
no work left undone.

Guide my hands, Jesus.
Fill my moments with You.
Then it makes no difference.
A year.
A day.
A moment.
I'll be ready, with everything completed.
No last minute preparations.
                  And no regrets.

Forty-Six

Jesus, they're burning people to death.
It's in the newspapers,
   on television,
      and in all its obscenity in weekly magazines.
Somewhere on the other side of the world
   men are firing bullets at other men
      and hitting children.
With marvelous chemical discoveries
      they consume whole villages in fire.
Houses,
   trees,
      grain,
         pigs,
           and babies
              blaze, then lie charred,
                 almost in an instant
                    —but not quite.
I'm sitting here,
   comfortable,
   watching a parade on television,
      becoming only slightly annoyed
      when the children's voices drown out the
                       bands.
They make the sounds of children.
   They laugh.
      They squabble over toys,
         clutter the room,

and blend a warm environment
of movement and child noise.
But somewhere on the other side of the world,
children are screaming.
Their shattered small hands
and arms
and legs
clutter detonated villages.
Fathers are dying,
deserting their families
in mass cremations
and shared graves.
Mothers, unmoving, are cradling grotesque infants,
holding in their arms, broken bodies
with dangling limbs
and opaque,
plastic eyes.

The parade is ending
and the children are becoming restless.
The bands were excellent.
But, Lord, I can't shut out those other sounds.
The screams are too loud.
And those other children,
those babies somewhere on the other side of the
world,
lying dismembered and charred,
are also my children.

Each is a member of my family
—and Yours.
They're my children,
my brothers,
my sisters,
my parents.
And they're being burned to death.

150

I'm sickened
    and frustrated
        and angry.
I want to do something
    but I don't know what to do.
Somehow, all the killing must be stopped.
I can't care about how it started,
    the discussion of rights and wrongs.
I can't listen to the endless arguments,
        the insane mouthings of politicians
            talking of international policy,
                casualty statistics,
                    and national images.
I can't hear them.
The screams are too loud.
Tell me what to do, Lord.
Show us the way to stop it.
    You're the only help we have.
Please listen, Jesus.
Little babies are being burned to death.
    And they're my children—

Forty-Seven

They say You're dead.
And maybe You are,
    at least some of the time,
        for them
        and for me.
I know there are times when I can't find You,
    times when You seem unreal,
        an abstraction,
          a myth,
            or even a neurosis.

But what of these other times,
    these moments when You are present,
        when You fill my room
        and Your voice is loud
          in my ears?

I look around and You are everywhere:
    in a blade of grass,
        the tear of a child,
          a hand in mine.
I find You in that soaring unity
    as our bodies join.
I see You in the single face of family prayer,
    hear Your song in the choir of children's voices,
        watch You walk the streets of our neighborhood
          and wander the darkened lanes of despair
                bringing light.

I watch You talk to people;
    I see Your words turn hate to love.
I glimpse Your face in the pleading eyes of hunger
    and watch Your hands reach out with food.
You,
    dead?
Then we have all lost life.
You die in us
    and all light goes out,
    all truth is gone
        and we are corpses
            rotting in a barren world.
No, You are not dead.
    Only I.
Each time I draw within,
    concern my thoughts with self
        and die to the world
        and love,
            I die to You.
Each time I set a limit
    and lock the doors on my family of the world,
        I kill a piece of me.
They say You're dead.
But no, You cannot die to me.
    You cannot cease to love.
              I can.
    And then I die,
        and You within me.

Forty-Eight

They're building a new church, Lord.
The walls and roof are up.
    Concrete blocks,
        steel reinforcing rods,
            massive laminated wood beams.
    All very modern,
        sterile,
            impressive,
                and costly.
They purchased land,
    brought in bulldozers,
        uprooted an orchard,
            and now they're building a church.
It's to be *our* church they are building.
But do You know something, Lord?
    I don't even know who *they* are!
We were told of the new church
    after the plans were drawn.
    We had no voice,
        but we were told it was to be *our* church.
But this doesn't annoy me, Lord.
Someone has to make the decisions
    and assume the responsibility.
It's something else that bothers me.
We're told it is our church,
    but where is our church?
        Where are the boundaries of our parish?

Are they limited by lines on a map of our
suburb?

I look around
    at our friends
        and neighbors,
            those who sit beside us in church.
Our families are well fed,
    perhaps even overfed;
Our children are clothed,
    educated,
        and loved.
We live in insulated houses,
    warmed in winter,
        cooled in summer.
        Secure.
We have automobiles
    and television sets
        and refrigerators
            and vacuum cleaners
                and king-size beds
                and books
                    and music
                        and comfort.

All in all,
    we have a very affluent parish.
But only if we are looking
    no further than the boundaries of a suburb.
And Lord, this can't be what You ask.
You taught us to be a family.
    By coming to us as our brother,
        You taught us to recognize all men
            as our brothers.
Where, then, is our church?
    The limits of our parish?

We have a letter from Africa, Jesus.

Their needs are basic,
    and acute.
They're members of our parish,
    aren't they?
And there are orphans in Hong Kong.
    They have little food,
        and little clothing.
Don't they also make up our family?

It's a very impressive church, Lord.
But what of all those others,
    those members of our parish
        outside the boundaries,
            all those You call Your brothers
                and ours?
Would they be impressed?
Are You?

Forty-Nine

Dear Lord, You called
    and we answered.
We embraced the vocation You offered.
    We said "I do."
And each day, again and again, we renew our pledge
        in words, in actions, with our bodies,
            and in the union of our souls
                    with You.

You hung, dear Jesus, lifeless in crucifixion.
    And You rose, glorified in resurrection.
You gave us life again
    and, in Your brotherhood, You returned us
                as children of Your Father.

You, our brother, what do You ask of us?
                What do You call us to?
Part of this life You have shown us,
    glimpses of its challenge.
Your voice has told us we are to witness
        Your union with Your Church.
            This is the call we heard,
                at first only faintly.

And this, Your call, we have answered.
We have succeeded in sanctity
        and failed in sin.

157

But always, Your voice has called us
　　　　　　　　　　　　back.

You've shared Your work,
　　　Your task of redemption,
　　　　　　　　　　with us.
You've called us to join You on the cross,
　　　　　　to die in You,
　　　　　　　　　　and rise again in Your glory.

Dear Lord, You came to us as *Love*.
You live in us as *Love*.
Help us, Jesus, to live this love.
Fill us with *You*.
Deepen the sexual love to which You have called us,
　　　　　Make of it a bond,
　　　　　　　a covenant with You.
　　　　　Sanctify it;
　　　　　　　let it rise as prayer.
　　　　　Shine through it, as sunlight through stained
　　　　　　　　　　　　　　　　glass,
　　　　　　　forming it, perfecting it,
　　　　　　　　in a transparency of You.
Show us how to love as You love.
Show us how to open our doors
　　　and pour out our love into the world.

Give us the courage, Christ Jesus, to give,
　　　　　always to give,
　　　　　　　more of Your love.
Deliver us from the temptation to lock out the world,
　　　　　to keep our life in love exclusive,
　　　　　　　hidden in a tower of comfort.
Give us the strength to hold to the promise.
Help us to make each day's "I do" a joyful
　　　　　　　acceptance of Your cross
　　　　　　　　as well as Your crown.

Listen to us, dearest Savior,
   You who have called us to a life in You
         and a union in each other,
   You, who have called us to walk in Your steps
         and to show forth Your love,
   live in us,
   shape us in Your image,
   fuse us in a oneness of spirit, intellect, and body.
   Make of us,
      Your brother and sister,
         a man and a woman "become one,"
      a unitary magnet
         drawing the world to You.